S0-BUA-839

SPOT THE DIFFERENCE

Find the 3 differences between the two pictures.

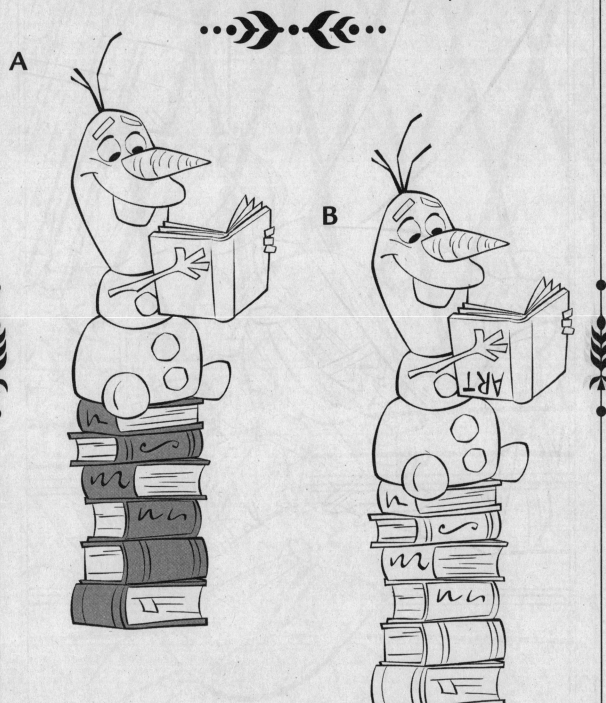

A

B

Answers: Book color, Missing ART, Missing stick.

© Disney

Anna wakes up to see the mysterious and beautiful northern lights. "The sky's awake. So I'm awake. So we have to play."

© Disney

Anna and Elsa have a bond like no other!

© Disney

WHICH PATH?

Which path leads Anna and Elsa to Sven and Kristoff?

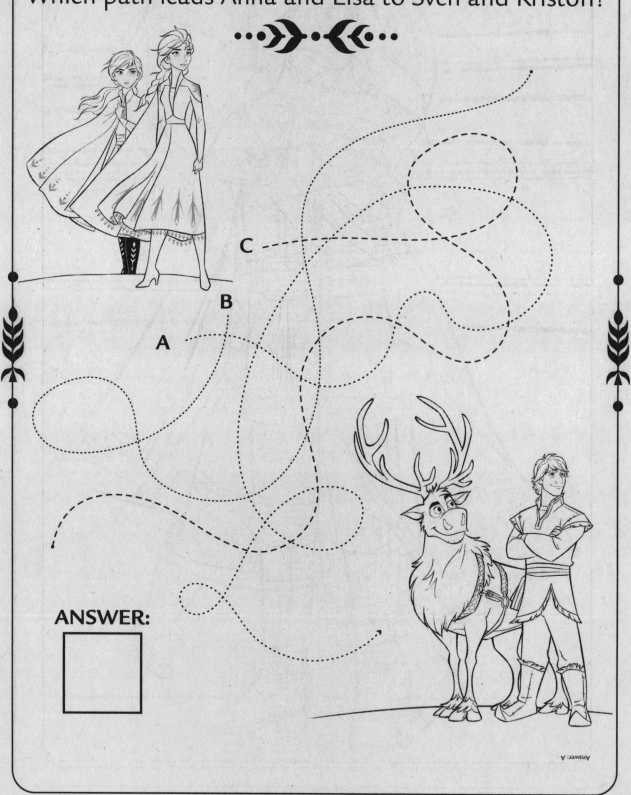

C

B

A

ANSWER:

Answer: A

© Disney

King Runeard was Anna and Elsa's grandfather.
He ruled Arendelle for many years.

© Disney

Elsa is queen of Arendelle. She always does
her best for the kingdom.

© Disney

Princess Anna loves everything about life in Arendelle.

© Disney

Olaf is ready for a new adventure!

© Disney

START

FINISH

Answer on last page.

© Disney

TIC-TAC-TOE

Elsa is ready for a challenge!

© Disney

Olaf has learned to read. He loves to learn all
about the world around him.

© Disney

Autumn has arrived in Arendelle!
Olaf helps Anna find the perfect pumpkin for the harvest table.

© Disney

CRACK THE CODE

Using the secret code below, fill in the blanks
to reveal the hidden message!

• • • • • •

A	B	C	D	E	F	G	H	I	J	K	L	M
1	2	3	4	5	6	7	8	9	10	11	12	13
N	O	P	Q	R	S	T	U	V	W	X	Y	Z
14	15	16	17	18	19	20	21	22	23	24	25	26

__ __ __ __ __ __
14 1 20 21 18 5

__ __
9 19

__ __ __ __ __ __ __
13 1 7 9 3 1 12

Answer: Nature is Magical!

© Disney

WORD SEARCH

Can you find the words in the grid below?

S	F	E	U	S	E	E	K	L
D	E	S	T	I	N	Y	C	F
M	A	G	I	C	A	L	H	O
Y	R	W	Q	R	P	B	V	R
T	L	M	G	I	K	W	Y	E
R	E	S	Q	V	F	X	J	S
D	S	Z	V	E	T	R	O	T
Z	S	P	I	R	I	T	S	I
N	O	R	T	H	A	U	N	X

Destiny   North   Spirits   Fearless

Forest   Magical   Seek   River

© Disney

Harvesting ice used to be Kristoff's life. Now he lives in Arendelle, surrounded by all his friends—including Anna, the love of his life.

© Disney

Sven is Kristoff's oldest friend.

© Disney

MISSING PIECE

Can you find the missing piece of the puzzle?

A

B

C

Answer: B

© Disney

LET'S DRAW

Use the grid below
to draw Anna.

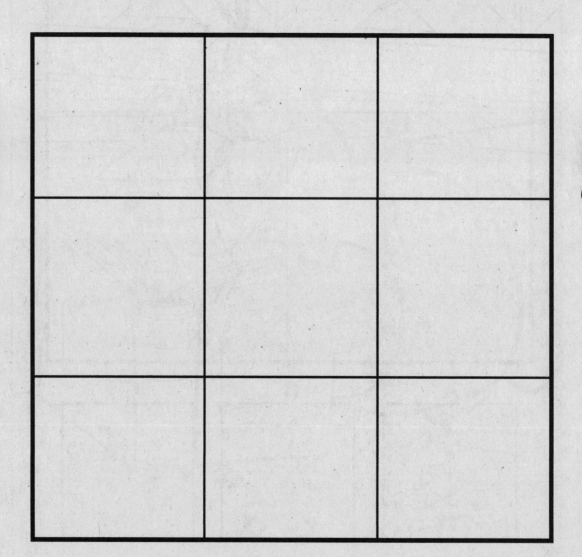

© Disney

Now that Olaf can read, he is full of fun facts and trivia.

© Disney

Olaf and Anna love warm hugs!

© Disney

BUILD-A-WORD

How many words can you make using the letters in:

STRONGER TOGETHER

EXAMPLE: Heroes

_____

_____

_____

_____

HINT:
You can use letters
more than once!

_____

_____

_____

_____

_____

_____

_____

© Disney

MATCHING

Which shadow is the correct match in each group?

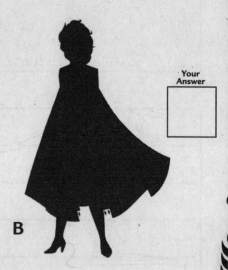

A

B

Your Answer

A

B

Your Answer

Answers: Top Group - A, Bottom Group - B

© Disney

Anna, Elsa, Kristoff, Sven, and Olaf play charades
for family game night.

© Disney

When Elsa feels sad, she wraps her mother's scarf around her shoulders.

© Disney

Anna will always be there for her sister.

© Disney

Elsa uses her powers and forms beautiful
ice crystals across the fjord.

© Disney

START

FINISH

Answer on last page.

© Disney

WHICH PATH?

Which path leads Elsa to Anna?

A

B

C

ANSWER:

Answer: B

© Disney

Anna can't believe what she is seeing!

© Disney

The trolls roll into town.

© Disney

Anna has never seen the trolls so far from
Valley of the Living Rock!

© Disney

Grand Pabbie senses a mysterious magic is at work.

© Disney

LET'S DRAW

Use the grid below
to draw Elsa.

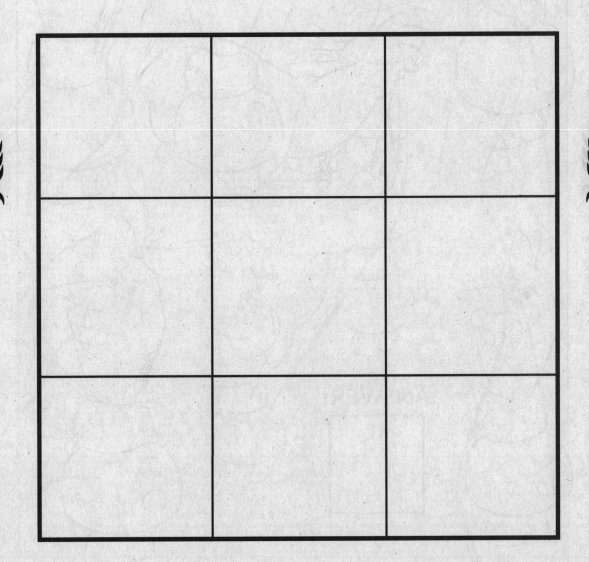

© Disney

HOW MANY?

How many pictures of Olaf do you see?

ANSWER:

© Disney

Answer: 8

Anna promises to go with Elsa and keep her safe,
no matter what.

© Disney

Elsa is ready to go to the Enchanted Forest!

© Disney

WORD SEARCH
Can you find the words in the grid below?

A	T	H	N	J	K	I	D	O
U	B	F	R	O	Z	E	N	C
T	S	H	Z	P	E	J	X	T
U	A	O	I	A	W	R	Y	R
M	E	M	O	R	I	E	S	U
N	L	E	D	H	N	O	Q	T
M	G	B	O	N	D	C	N	H
K	U	N	A	T	U	R	E	F
L	W	P	V	F	M	E	B	G

Autumn   Bond   Nature   Frozen

Wind   Memories   Truth   Home

© Disney

SPOT THE DIFFERENCE

Find the 3 differences between the two pictures.

A

B

Answers: Cape color, Dress color, Snowflake on shoulder

© Disney

Anna will do anything to help her sister.

© Disney

Sven is always happy to help his friends.

© Disney

TIC-TAC-TOE

Anna is ready for a challenge!

© Disney

MISSING PIECE

Can you find the missing piece of the puzzle?

A

B
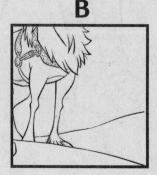

C

Answer: B

© Disney

Kristoff is ready to travel north.

© Disney

They will take Kristoff's wagon to journey far beyond Arendelle.

© Disney

A-MAZE-ING

Lead Anna through the maze to find Olaf.

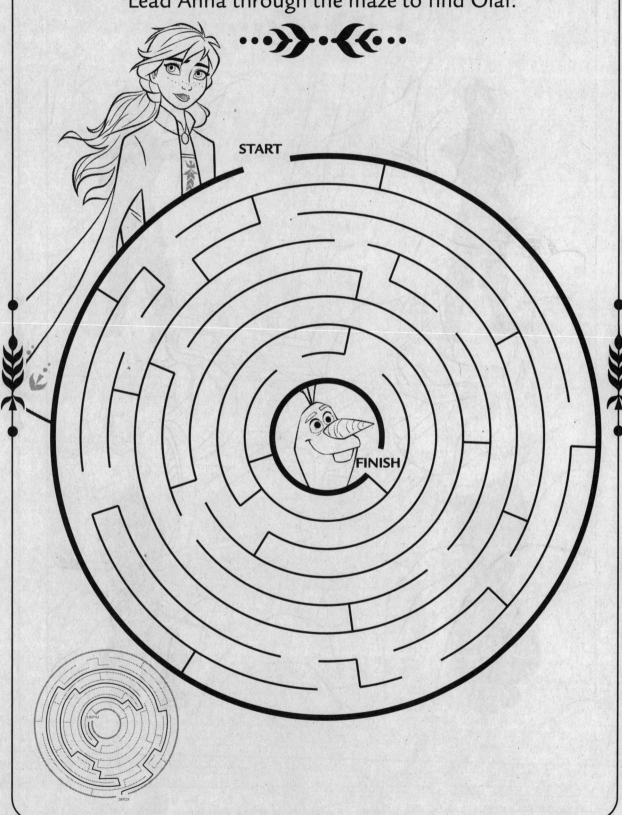

START

FINISH

© Disney

MATCHING

Which shadow is the correct match in each group?

A

B

A

B

Answers: Top Group - B, Bottom Group - A

© Disney

On the way to the Enchanted Forest, the friends pass Elsa's ice palace. They are traveling farther north than ever before!

© Disney

During their long journey, Olaf entertains his
friends with fun facts.

© Disney

Anna and Elsa spot something in the distance.

© Disney

Elsa discovers giant monoliths.

© Disney

Each monolith has one of
four symbols: fire, water, wind, and earth.

© Disney

The friends enter the mist that surrounds the Enchanted Forest.
It traps them inside!

© Disney

HOW MANY?

How many pictures of Sven do you see?

ANSWER:

Answer: 7

© Disney

WHICH PATH?

Which path leads Olaf to Elsa?

C

B

A

ANSWER:

© Disney

Answer: C

Elsa uses her magic in the Enchanted Forest.

© Disney

Olaf loves leaping into large piles of leaves!

© Disney

start

finish

Answer on last page.

© Disney

MISSING PIECE

Can you find the missing piece of the puzzle?

A

B

C

Answer: C

© Disney

Olaf and Sven are amazed by the beauty of the forest.

© Disney

Olaf is busy exploring the Enchanted Forest.

© Disney

TIC-TAC-TOE

Kristoff and Sven are ready for a challenge!

© Disney

A strange wind surrounds Anna. It's the Wind Spirit!

© Disney

The Wind Spirit notices Elsa's magic.

© Disney

HOW MANY?

How many pictures of the Fire Spirit do you see?

ANSWER:

© Disney

Answer: 7

Elsa is unsure what awaits her in the Enchanted Forest.

© Disney

Anna and Elsa are happy to see each other.

© Disney

SPOT THE DIFFERENCE

Find the 3 differences between the two pictures.

A

B

Answers: Belt color, shoe color, pants color.

© Disney

Anna and Elsa are caught up by the Wind Spirit!

© Disney

The Wind Spirit is powerful! What does it want?

© Disney

Elsa uses her powers to slow down the Wind Spirit.
She frees everyone and forms ice sculptures.

© Disney

DO YOU WANT TO BUILD A SNOWMAN?

Draw your own snowman in the space below.

© Disney

© Disney

CRACK THE CODE

Using the secret code below, fill in the blanks
to reveal the hidden message!

• • • • • •

A	B	C	D	E	F	G	H	I	J	K	L	M
1	2	3	4	5	6	7	8	9	10	11	12	13
N	O	P	Q	R	S	T	U	V	W	X	Y	Z
14	15	16	17	18	19	20	21	22	23	24	25	26

___ ___ ___
20   8   5

___ ___ ___ ___ ___ ___ ___
10   15   21   18   14   5   25

___ ___ ___ ___ ___ ___ ___ ___
3   15   14   14   5   3   20   19

___ ___
21   19

Answer: The Journey Connects Us

Elsa is prepared to use her magic.

© Disney

Anna and Elsa will always be there for each other.

© Disney

MATCHING

Which shadow correctly matches Anna?

A

ANSWER:

B

Answer: A

© Disney

TIC-TAC-TOE

Olaf is ready for a challenge!

Anna recognizes Lieutenant Mattias. "Library, second portrait on the left. You were our father's official guard."

© Disney

These Arendellian soldiers have been trapped
in the forest a long time.

© Disney

They have sworn to protect Arendelle, no matter what.

© Disney

start

finish

Answer on last page.

© Disney

TRUE
to Myself

© Disney

Yelana is Northuldra. The Northuldra have been trapped in the Enchanted Forest for thirty-four years.

© Disney

LET'S DRAW

Use the grid below
to draw Kristoff.

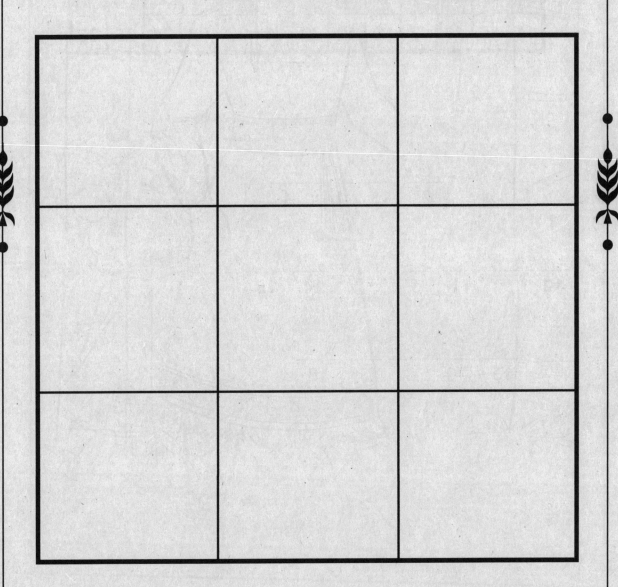

© Disney

CRACK THE CODE

Using the secret code below, fill in the blanks
to reveal the hidden message!

• • • • • •

A	B	C	D	E	F	G	H	I	J	K	L	M
1	2	3	4	5	6	7	8	9	10	11	12	13
N	O	P	Q	R	S	T	U	V	W	X	Y	Z
14	15	16	17	18	19	20	21	22	23	24	25	26

___   ___ ___ ___ ___
1   2   15   14   4

___ ___ ___ ___   ___ ___
12   9   11   5   14   15

___ ___ ___ ___ ___
15   20   8   5   18

Answer: A Bond Like No Other

© Disney

Honeymaren is also Northuldra. She has spent her entire life trapped inside the Enchanted Forest.

© Disney

Ryder and Honeymaren are brother and sister.

© Disney

Honeymaren wonders what life is like
outside the Enchanted Forest.

© Disney

The Northuldra are reindeer herders. Ryder can't wait to see the open plains outside the Enchanted Forest.

© Disney

Ryder and Sven are friends already!

© Disney

Olaf is happy to make new friends in the Enchanted Forest.

© Disney

MAGICAL JOURNEY!

Draw yourself on a magical journey in the space below.

• • • • • • •

© Disney

The Fire Spirit appears!
It races through the forest, lighting small fires.

© Disney

Kristoff and Sven race off to save
the reindeer from the Fire Spirit.

© Disney

WORD UNSCRAMBLE

Unscramble the words below.

THIMCY

_____

DENDHI

_____

IIRTPSS

_____

ARNTEU

_____

Answers: Mythic, Hidden, Spirits, Nature

© Disney

The Fire Spirit is a small salamander.

© Disney

The Fire Spirit likes Elsa's cold touch.

© Disney

Elsa conjures small snowflakes for the Fire Spirit.

© Disney

The Fire Spirit is named Bruni.

© Disney© Disney

BUILD-A-WORD

How many words can you make using the letters in:
WILDERNESS MAN

HINT:
*You can use letters
more than once!*

EXAMPLE: REINDEER

© Disney

SPOT THE DIFFERENCE

Find the 3 differences between the two pictures.

© Disney

Answers: Fire, Leaf, Pattern

Elsa made Olaf permafrost. Now he won't melt!

© Disney

Kristoff and Sven grew up in nature.

© Disney

Sven runs through the forest with his new reindeer friends.

© Disney

A-MAZE-ING

Lead Ryder through the maze to find Honeymaren.

START

FINISH

© Disney

© Disney

Mattias shares his wisdom with Anna.
"Don't give up, take it one step at a time, and . . ."
"Just do the right thing?" Anna finishes.

© Disney

WHICH PATH?

Which path leads Elsa to the Water Nokk?

C

B

A

ANSWER:

Answer: C

© Disney

Olaf and Sven have a special friendship.

© Disney

Ryder has an idea to help Kristoff surprise Anna.
It involves a lot of reindeer!

© Disney

start

finish

Answer on last page.

© Disney

Honeymaren explains the symbols on Elsa's mother's scarf.

© Disney

Boom, boom, boom! The Earth Giants appear.

© Disney

MATCHING
Which shadow is the correct match?

A

B

ANSWER:

Answer: B

© Disney

WORD SEARCH

Can you find the words in the grid below?

```
S D K A N N A X L L
C K W C B O L A F
T R O L L S R E K
V I M E J B E L D
F S I S T E R S P
N T I J S I O A F
J O U R N E Y T O
H F A Z O M G A L
U F G N W Y P H Q
```

Elsa Anna Olaf Kristoff

Trolls Snow Sister Journey

© Disney

Anna tries to draw the Earth Giants' attention.

© Disney

The Earth Giants roam the Enchanted Forest at night.

© Disney

MISSING PIECE

Can you find the missing piece of the puzzle?

A

B

C

Answer: C

© Disney

WORD UNSCRAMBLE

Unscramble the words below.

SENV

_____

NAAN

_____

SELA

_____

LFOA

_____

Answers: Sven, Anna, Elsa, and Olaf

© Disney

© Disney

Olaf has lots of questions.
The more he reads and learns, the more questions he has!

Anna is happy to see that Elsa is safe.

© Disney

BUILD-A-WORD

How many words can you make using the letters in:

MAGICAL JOURNEY

HINT:
*You can use letters
more than once!*

EXAMPLE: Crayon

_____   _____

_____   _____

_____   _____

_____   _____

_____   _____

_____   _____

_____   _____

© Disney

SQUARES

Taking turns, connect a line from one star to another. If you draw a line that completes a square, write your initial in the square. The person with the most squares at the end of the game wins!

• • • • • •

© Disney

Anna and Olaf refuse to let Elsa go off on her own.
"We do this together."

© Disney

Elsa sends Anna and Olaf away to safety in an ice boat.

© Disney

Anna promises never to leave Olaf. "Pinky swear."

© Disney

Shhhh! Anna and Olaf can't make a sound or they will wake up the sleeping Earth Giants!

© Disney

Anna turns the ice boat toward a waterfall. "Hang on, Olaf."

© Disney

Olaf always looks on the bright side.

© Disney

TIC-TAC-TOE

Ryder is ready for a challenge!

© Disney

LET'S DRAW

Use the grid below to draw Olaf.

© Disney

Anna and Olaf explore the Lost Caverns.

© Disney

Elsa stands on the black sand beach at the edge of the Dark Sea.
She uses her magic to try to find a way across the fierce waves.

© Disney

SPOT THE DIFFERENCE
Find the 3 differences between the two pictures.

A

B

Answers: Leaf from belt, stripe on pants, cape is colored

© Disney

MISSING PIECE
Can you find the missing piece of the puzzle?

A

B

C

Answer: A

© Disney

Perched on a tall rock, Elsa prepares to cross the Dark Sea.

© Disney

Elsa uses her ice powers to race across the crashing waves.

© Disney

HOW MANY?

How many pictures of Anna do you see?

ANSWER:

Answer: 6

© Disney

MATCHING

Which shadow is the correct match?

A

B

ANSWER:

Answer: A

© Disney

The Water Nokk is a fierce warrior that
emerges from the Dark Sea.

© Disney

A-MAZE-ING

Lead Elsa through the maze to find Anna.

START

FINISH

© Disney

BACK ON THE
Trails

© Disney

The Water Nokk challenges Elsa.

© Disney

Elsa faces the Water Nokk beneath the waves!

© Disney

HOW MANY?

How many pictures of the Water Nokk do you see?

ANSWER:

Answer: 9

© Disney

Anna will always be true to herself.

© Disney

FEARLESS
by Nature

© Disney

SPOT THE DIFFERENCE

Find the 3 differences between the two pictures.

A

B

Answers: Sleeve color, pattern on boot missing, pattern on cape missing

© Disney

A-MAZE-ING

Lead Kristoff through the maze to find Olaf.

START

FINISH

© Disney

Elsa has successfully crossed the Dark Sea!

© Disney

Anna is prepared to do the next right thing.

© Disney

MISSING PIECE

Can you find the missing piece of the puzzle?

A

B

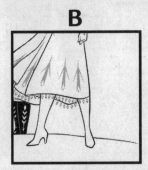

C

Answer: A

© Disney

ANSWER KEY

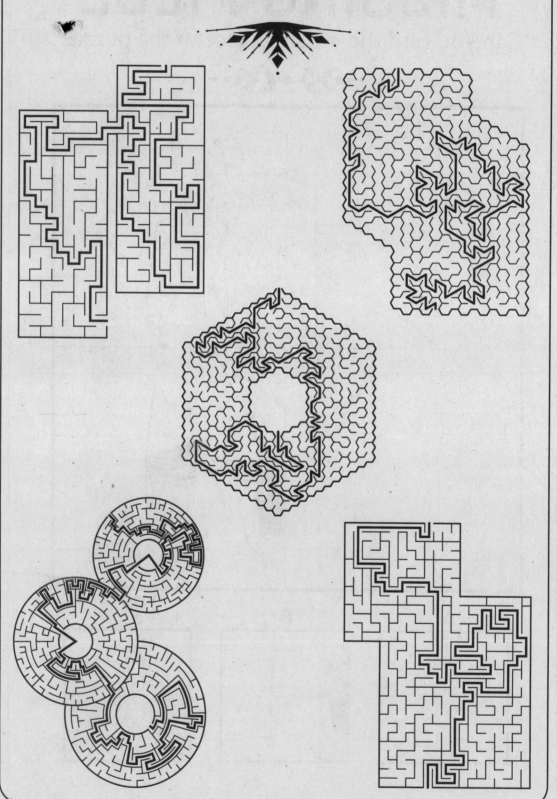

© Disney